AUTHOR DEDICATION
*For Bryn Kelly (This isn't the answer
to your question, but it's close enough.)*

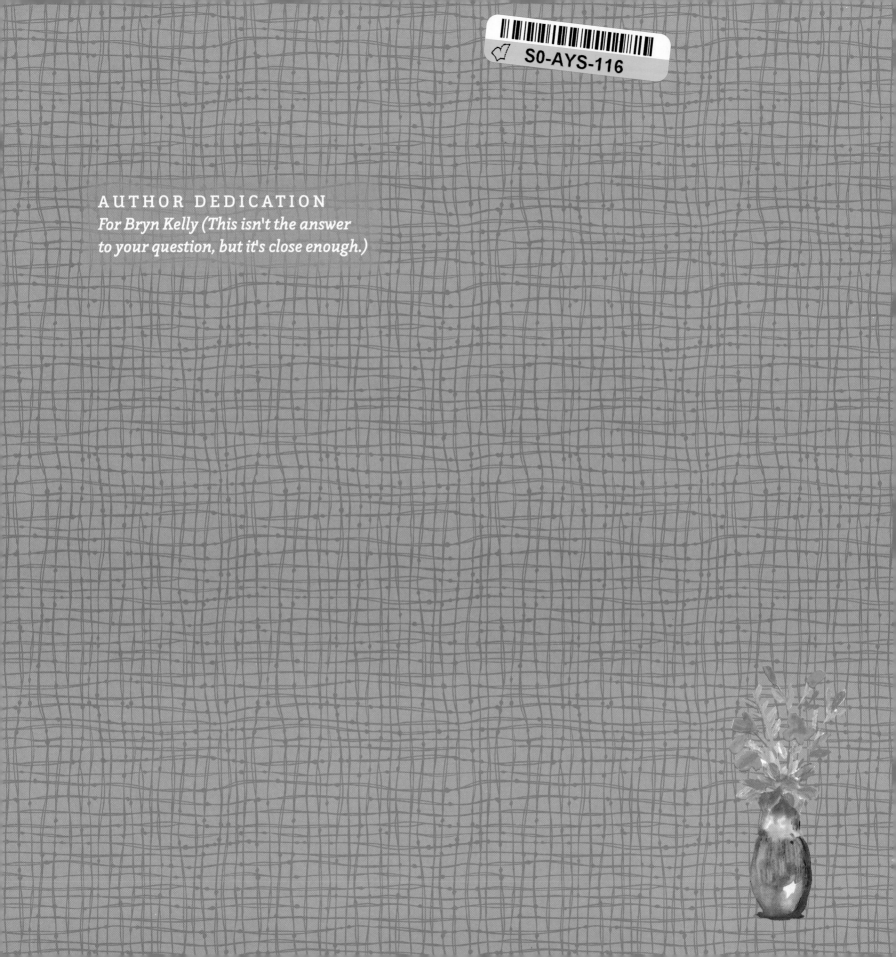

Reycraft Books
55 Fifth Avenue
New York, NY 10003
Reycraftbooks.com

Reycraft Books is a trade imprint and trademark of Newmark Learning, LLC.

Library of Congress Cataloging-in-Publication Data is available.

ISBN: 978-1-4788-6862-0

Illustration credit: Luciano Lozano

Photograph credits: Jacket (front, texture), Jacket (back), Cover (texture), Title Page (red texture), Back Cover (background) © crabgarden/Shutterstock; Pages i, ii, iii, 32–35 (background) © Mikhaylova Liubov/Shutterstock; Page 32 (author photo) courtesy of Charles Ludeke.

Printed in Guangzhou, China
4401/0220/CA22000111
10 9 8 7 6 5 4 3 2

First Edition Hardcover published by Reycraft Books

Call Me Max

BY KYLE LUKOFF • ILLUSTRATED BY LUCIANO LOZANO

Chapter 1

When I look in the mirror I see a boy.

I see a boy with spiky brown hair.

I see a boy with white skin that tans in the summer.

I see a boy with one mom
and one dad
and two goldfish.

I also see a boy who is transgender.

TRANSGENDER is a long word.

But it means something simple.

TRANS means going across.
Like how transportation
means going from

HERE

TO
THERE.

GENDER means being
a boy or a girl.

Or a little of both.

Or not feeling like a boy or a girl.

When a baby is born, a grown-up says,

"IT'S A BOY!" or "IT'S A GIRL!"

If a brand-new baby could talk,
sometimes that baby might say,

"NO I'M NOT!"

When a baby grows up to be transgender, it means that the grown-up
who said they were a boy or a girl made a mistake.

When I was born, my mom and dad said, "It's a girl!"
When I looked in the mirror, I saw a girl.

Kind of.

But because I'm transgender, I wanted to see a boy.

My parents thought it was cute when I put on my dad's ties.

I liked to sleep in my Batman shirt.

When they bought me a dress for my first day of school,

I lost it.

I didn't tell them I lost it at the bottom of the garbage can.

I wore my favorite overalls instead.

I thought school would be hard
because I didn't know how to read.

I thought school would be hard
because I wouldn't get to play all day.

But school turned out to be hard for other reasons.

Chapter 2

On the first day of school, the teacher
called out our names.

"Emory?" "Here!"

"Stella?" "Me!"

I raised my hand when she got to my name.
She looked at me.
And then at the list of names.
And then back at me again.

I wondered if she thought my name didn't make sense for me.
I felt that way too.

"Can you call me Max?" I asked.

Max is the boy in my favorite book.

She nodded and wrote it down.

(I won't tell you what my old name was.

That's private.)

I had to go to the bathroom after snack.

At home there is one bathroom for everyone to use.

When I went to the store with my dad,

I went into the bathroom with him.

When I went to the movies with my mom,

I went into the bathroom with her.

But at school I had to pick which bathroom to use.

When I went in the girls' bathroom, a girl ran out.
She thought I was a boy. I didn't mean to scare her.
But I liked that she thought I was a boy.

I used the boys'
bathroom instead.
But when I came
out I saw kids
giggling and
pointing.

16

I decided to hold it all day.
And tried not to drink too much water,
no matter how thirsty I got.

Chapter 3

Making friends was easy.

But everyone asked if I was a boy or a girl.

I told my friend Teresa that I wanted to be a boy.

She asked me why.

"Because I like climbing trees," I told her.

"And looking for gross bugs."

She looked mad.

"I'm a girl," she told me.
"And we climbed this tree together!
I also caught more spiders
than you did."

"Oh yeah," I said. "Sorry. I forgot.
But spiders aren't bugs.
And I still don't think I'm a girl."

"I know spiders aren't bugs," Teresa said.
"Why don't you think you're a girl?"

"Because I don't feel like one on the inside."

21

I told my friend Steven that I might be a boy.
"I can't be a girl," I said.
"I hate wearing dresses."

He looked down at his dress, and then glared at me.
"This is my favorite dress. And I like being a boy."

"Oh yeah," I said. "I forgot. I'm sorry. And it's a pretty dress.
But I still know I'm a boy."

"How come?" he asked.

"Because I feel like one," I told him.
"On the inside."

Chapter 4

One day Steven and Teresa came over to play.
My parents heard them call me Max.

During dinner they asked me why. I told them all about school.
How I couldn't go to the bathroom. How I didn't like my old name.
How I felt like a boy.

My mom and dad talked to my teacher,
and we found a group for kids like me.
Boys and girls, and kids who weren't boys or girls.
All of us were transgender.
We talked about serious things,
like bathrooms and teasing.
We also talked about fun things,
like video games and books and toys.

I don't know what our parents talked about.
Probably the same things.

I told my class that I was transgender.

The boys got used to having me in their bathroom.

The girls didn't want me in theirs anyway.

Teresa and I kept climbing trees and finding gross bugs.

I still didn't want to play dress-up with Steven.

Some of the girls in the group gave me their old boy clothes.
I gave them some of my old girl clothes.

Being a boy isn't better than being a girl. But being myself is the best.

Kyle Lukoff has worked at the intersection of books and people for over half his life, first as a bookseller, then as a school librarian, and now as a writer. He is transgender, like Max, and lives in a small Brooklyn apartment with six overflowing bookshelves.

Luciano Lozano was born the same year Man traveled to the Moon. That may be the reason why he has traveled a lot since childhood. When not traveling he lives in Barcelona. His illustrations reflect his strong sense of color and texture, as well as his subtle sense of humor.